UP CLOSE

DESERT

WILDLIFE

GW00731530

JOSHUA MORRIS PUBLISHING

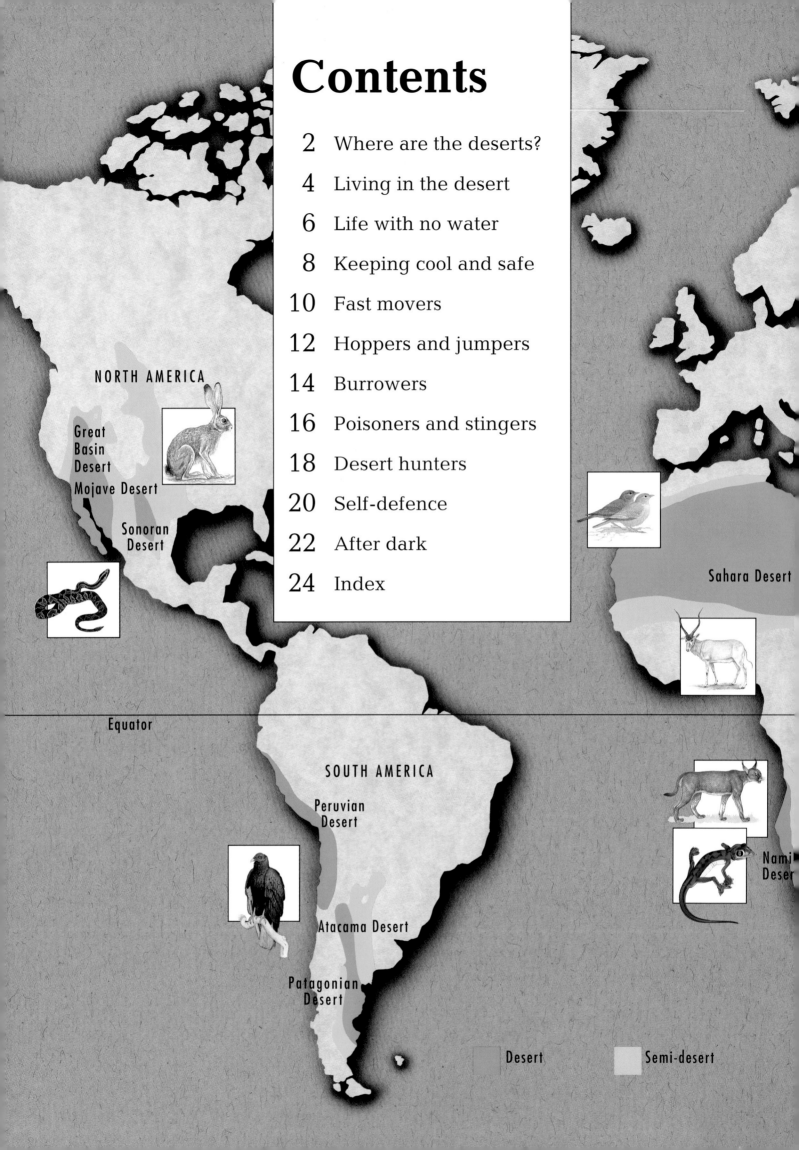

Contents

NORTH AMERICA

Great
Basin
Desert

Mojave Desert

Sonoran
Desert

Sahara Desert

Equator

SOUTH AMERICA

Peruvian
Desert

Atacama Desert

Patagonian
Desert

Nami
Deser

Desert   Semi-desert

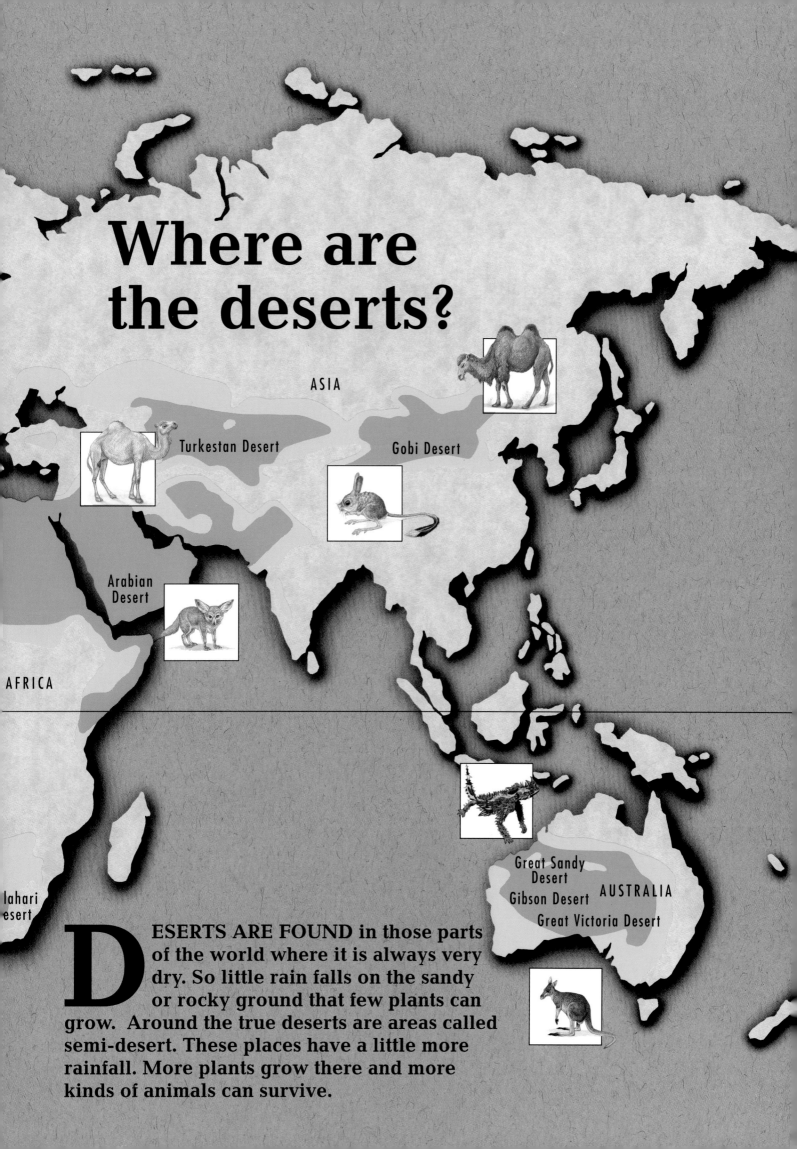

Where are the deserts?

ASIA

Turkestan Desert

Gobi Desert

Arabian
Desert

AFRICA

Kalahari
Desert

Great Sandy
Desert
Gibson Desert   AUSTRALIA
Great Victoria Desert

DESERTS ARE FOUND in those parts of the world where it is always very dry. So little rain falls on the sandy or rocky ground that few plants can grow. Around the true deserts are areas called semi-desert. These places have a little more rainfall. More plants grow there and more kinds of animals can survive.

Living in the desert

DESERTS MAY BE hard places to live in, but they are certainly not empty. Many animals and plants survive despite the harsh conditions. Deserts near the equator are hot during the day all year round. But deserts farther away from the equator, such as the Gobi Desert in Asia, are bitterly cold in winter.

Key

These are some of the animals and plants that live in deserts. They come from all over the world and, in reality, would not all be seen together.

1	Meerkat	8	Sidewinder	13	Jerboa
2	Saguaro cactus	9	Prickly pear	14	Scorpion
3	Cactus wren	10	Fennec fox	15	Thorny devil
4	Lappet-faced vulture	11	Gecko	16	Red-kneed
5	Locusts	12	Diamondback		tarantula
6	Dromedary camel		rattlesnake		
7	Great gerbil				

Life with no water

The **addax** never seems to drink. It gets all the water it needs from the plants it eats. The addax is particularly good at finding patches of desert plants that spring up after a sudden shower.

PLANTS AND ANIMALS need water to stay alive. And finding enough water in the desert is life's biggest problem. Some desert plants have very long roots that spread out to find water. Many desert animals can live for days without actually drinking. They can get enough water from their food.

The male **sand grouse** flies to a water hole, often travelling a long way to find one. He wades in, and special feathers on his breast soak up water like a sponge. He flies back to the nest where thirsty chicks suck water from his feathers.

Folds of skin in the **chuckwalla** lizard's sides contain special glands in which liquid can be stored. This stored liquid can keep the lizard alive through a long dry seaon.

GUESS WHAT?...

The darkling beetle survives in the desert by drinking dew.

This beetle lives in the Namib Desert, on the coast of southern Africa. It hardly ever rains there, but in the mornings fog rolls in from the sea, leaving dew on the beetle's body. The beetle then stands on its head and drinks the drops of dew that roll down its back.

Like many desert animals, the Australian **mulgara** has very concentrated urine that helps it retain as much water as possible. The mulgara rarely drinks but gets liquid from the juicy insects and lizards it eats.

When it does rain in the desert, cacti, such as this **organ-pipe cactus**, store up as much water as possible in their large, fleshy stems. This storage system helps the plants stay alive during long dry periods.

A **dromedary camel** can go for days, even weeks, without drinking. But when it does find water, it can drink more than 100 litres in a few minutes.

Desert **hedgehogs** get moisture from food such as birds' eggs. They also feed on deadly scorpions—but only after nipping off their poisonous stings.

Keeping cool and safe

WHEN DANGER threatens, the desert does not have many hiding places. Instead, desert creatures have found other ways of keeping safe. Many are sandy coloured, almost matching their surroundings, and so it is hard for hunting animals to see them. Insects and other small creatures hide underground in the sand.

With little shelter it is easy for animals to become too hot. Many have pale-coloured bodies that reflect the sun — dark colours absorb more heat.

Desert larks have dark or light brown feathers, depending on the colour of the rocks or sand where they live. This helps them hide from enemies, such as desert cats and foxes.

The pale feathers of the **cream-coloured courser** blend with the colour of the desert sands and help keep it hidden. This bird usually runs rather than flies, grabbing insects in its sharp beak.

The big ears of the **rabbit-eared bandicoot** help it stay cool. Its ears give off heat—just like a radiator. This bandicoot digs up insects to eat with its strong claws.

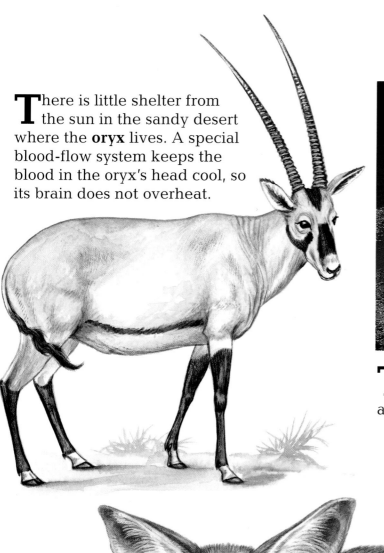

There is little shelter from the sun in the sandy desert where the **oryx** lives. A special blood-flow system keeps the blood in the oryx's head cool, so its brain does not overheat.

Trees need to keep cool too. **Eucalyptus trees** have white bark that reflects the sun and so keeps the trees from getting too hot.

Like the bandicoot, the **fennec fox** has big ears that keep it cool. These ears also pick up the slightest sound, helping the fox find prey.

The desert sandfish is really a lizard, but it does 'swim' through the sand.

This little creature burrows into the sand and wriggles along so fast that it almost seems to swim along. Its sandy colour helps keep it hidden from enemies as it hunts for beetles and other insects to eat.

GUESS WHAT?...

Fast movers

SOFT, SHIFTING SAND can make it difficult to get about quickly. But many desert animals have special ways of moving fast. Some snakes and lizards wriggle along, almost as though they are swimming through the sand. Many desert birds have long, slender toes to help spread their weight on the sandy soil. Other desert-living creatures, like the pronghorn, are perfectly designed for fast running on the flat, open land.

The **sand cat** has thick fur, even on the soles of its feet. This helps it move quickly on the sand, protecting it from the heat.

A trail of parallel marks in the sand is the sign of the **sidewinder**. This snake moves by throwing its body into two loops that it then pushes against the ground to move sideways.

Even when only a few days old, the **pronghorn** can run faster than an adult human. And a fully grown pronghorn can keep up a speed of nearly 50 kilometres an hour to escape from its enemies.

The **ostrich**, the largest bird in the world, cannot fly, but it is a fast runner. It can race along at speeds of more than 70 kilometres an hour.

Second only to the ostrich in size, the **emu** is also a speedy bird. It races across the Australian desert in search of food such as berries, grass and insects.

The webbed feet of this little **gecko** act like snowshoes, helping it move swiftly over the soft sand. The gecko's long legs keep its body well above the baking-hot ground.

GUESS WHAT?...

The greater roadrunner can fly but usually runs very fast after its prey.

Although only 50 centimetres long, this bird can run at a speed of 20 kilometres an hour. An expert at catching snakes, the roadrunner grabs its victim just behind the head to avoid getting bitten. It also eats mice, lizards and spiders.

Hoppers and jumpers

BOUNDING AND HOPPING movements are well suited to the wide-open spaces of the desert, where there are few trees and bushes to get in an animal's way. Some tiny creatures such as gerbils, jerboas and kangaroo rats move just like miniature kangaroos—they hop on their two strong back legs instead of running on four legs. Most of these animals have a long tail that helps them keep their balance.

The **black-tailed jackrabbit** can hop along on its long back legs as well as run fast on all fours. It can move at about 50 kilometres an hour for short periods.

The **large North African gerbil's** long back legs and feet help it bound along and also keep its body well off the burning sand.

Some wallabies live in forests, but the **spectacled hare wallaby** spends its life in the Australian desert. It eats the few tough, spiny plants that grow there.

The back legs of the **great jerboa**—an excellent jumper—are at least four times the size of its front legs. It eats seeds and insects, which it finds by combing through the sand with the long claws on its front feet.

Desert **kangaroo rats** sleep by day and come out at night to find seeds and insects to eat. Like hamsters, they have cheek pouches in which they carry food.

GUESS WHAT?...

Although a red kangaroo is bigger than an adult human, its newborn baby is only a few centimetres long.

The female kangaroo carries this tiny baby in the pouch at the front of her body as she bounds along on strong back legs.

The little **grasshopper mouse** catches scorpions and other insects to eat, but it may sometimes attack other mice.

Burrowers

DESERTS MAY SEEM empty, but many creatures spend much of their lives hidden in cool, dark burrows just below the surface. Even a few centimetres down, temperatures are lower and the air a little more moist—a welcome relief from the dry heat of the daytime sun. Once in its burrow, the animal is also safe from desert cats, hawks and other hunters.

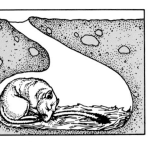

Kangaroo rats and spiders are among the many creatures that live in underground burrows in the desert.

The little **kowari** is a marsupial—it has a pouch like a kangaroo. It lives in burrows, alone or in small groups, and comes out at night to hunt for lizards and insects to eat.

Great gerbils live in the Gobi Desert, where winters are cold. In summer, the gerbils build up stores of plant food in their burrows to help them survive the winter.

Even snakes live in burrows. The **burrowing viper** digs into the soil with its strong snout and usually comes out only at night. It eats small creatures such as lizards, which it kills with its poisonous bite.

Burrowing owls lay their eggs in burrows, often those left by other animals. But they can also dig their own burrows, using their strong beaks as well as their long legs.

Because it lives in sandy areas, the **marsupial mole** cannot make permanent burrows. But with the help of its shovel-like forepaws, it tunnels through the sand, searching for earthworms to eat.

Spadefoot toads live in burrows, but when the rare rains do come, the toads come out to lay their eggs in rainwater pools.

GUESS WHAT?...

These honeypot ants are living storage pots.

Special workers in a honeypot ant colony are filled with food by other ants until they can hardly move. They then hang upside down in the ants' underground nest until a time of food shortage. Then their stores are used by the whole colony.

Poisoners and stingers

SOME OF THE MOST poisonous of all creatures live in the desert. There are scorpions, spiders, snakes—and even a poisonous lizard. These creatures use their venomous bites and stings to kill their prey. Food can be hard to find in the desert, and it is useful to be able to kill a victim quickly before it has a chance to escape. A desert animal may also use its poison to defend itself against enemies.

The **diamondback rattlesnake** is one of the most dangerous snakes in North America. It kills its prey by injecting deadly poison through its two sharp, hollow fangs.

Black widow spiders live in all warm regions of the world, as well as in deserts. They eat insects, such as flies and beetles, and even other spiders, which they catch in their sticky webs.

Saw-scaled adders kill more people than any other snake. But they only bite people in self-defence. Normally the snakes hunt mice, lizards and insects.

GUESS WHAT?...

The poison of the Sahara Desert scorpion is so strong that it has even killed people.

The scorpion's sting is at the end of its tail. The scorpion grabs its victim in its pincers, then curves the sting over its back to deliver the poison.

It may look fierce, but the **red-kneed tarantula** is harmless to humans. It eats insects and small creatures such as lizards, which it kills with its poisonous bite.

Brilliant **red velvet mites** are highly poisonous. Although less than a centimetre long, velvet mites have even been known to kill mice.

The brightly coloured **gila monster** is one of only two poisonous lizards in the world. It kills its prey with a venomous bite. It stores fat in its stumpy tail and lives on this when food is scarce.

Desert hunters

ALTHOUGH SOME ANIMALS manage to survive on desert plants and seeds, many live by hunting and eating other animals. There are several species of cats in the desert, as well as foxes, hyenas and hunting birds. Most of these hunters can run or fly swiftly and have sharp teeth or claws for killing prey.

Like all vultures, the **lappet-faced vulture** is a scavenger. It searches for dead animals to eat, or finishes off prey that other hunters have killed.

A fierce hunter, the **red-tailed hawk** watches for rabbits and lizards from a perch on a high branch or cactus. It also chases other birds in flight.

The long-legged **caracal** moves fast to pounce on creatures such as lizards, mice and young antelope. It also climbs trees or leaps into the air to catch birds.

Teamwork is the secret of the meerkats' success. Some go hunting while others keep guard or care for the young.

The meerkat is a type of mongoose and lives in family groups of ten to thirty animals. Each meerkat in the group has its own duties. Sentries watch for birds of prey—their main enemies—while other meerkats hunt for small creatures such as lizards, birds and even snakes.

A small, slender fox with large ears, the **kit fox** hunts at night. It searches for lizards, mice and other small creatures.

Whether hunting alone or in packs, **dingoes** often travel many kilometres across the desert in search of food. They are relatives of the domestic dogs first brought to Australia thousands of years ago.

Self-defence

HEAT AND LACK of water are not the only difficulties in the lives of desert animals. They also have to protect themselves against the prowling predators that try to catch them. There are few places to hide, so many desert creatures have other ways of keeping safe. Some, such as the skunk, smell so bad that they put off any would-be hunter. Others are too spiny to eat.

The bright colours of many desert animals, like lizards, also serve as a warning for enemies to stay clear.

The huge **Gould's monitor lizard**, also known as **Gould's goanna**, is up to 1.5 metres long—probably bigger than you. It makes itself look fiercer by standing up on its hind legs to threaten its enemies. This Australian lizard hunts for birds, insects and even other lizards.

The **barrel cactus** is well suited to desert life. It can store water inside its rounded shape to keep itself alive during long dry periods. And its spiny leaves protect it from plant-eating animals.

The thorny devil, a type of lizard that lives in the Australian desert, is as spiny as a cactus plant.

Few animals would dare to attack this creature, even though it is slow-moving and easy to catch. Its body bristles with large, sharp spines from its head to the tip of its tail. Even newly-hatched baby thorny devils are covered with spines.

Cactus wrens find their food on the ground. They nest on spiny cactus plants to keep their eggs safe from hunters.

The **pancake tortoise** has a very soft, flat shell. When in danger, it hides in a rock crevice. It then puffs up its body by breathing in lots of air so that it becomes firmly wedged in the rocks.

Like all skunks, the **spotted skunk** defends itself from enemies by squirting them with a strong-smelling liquid. This comes from glands under the skunk's tail and smells so bad that it makes it hard for the victim to breathe.

Prickly pear cacti are among the spiniest of all desert plants and almost impossible for animals to eat. These spines are, in fact, very tiny leaves.

After dark

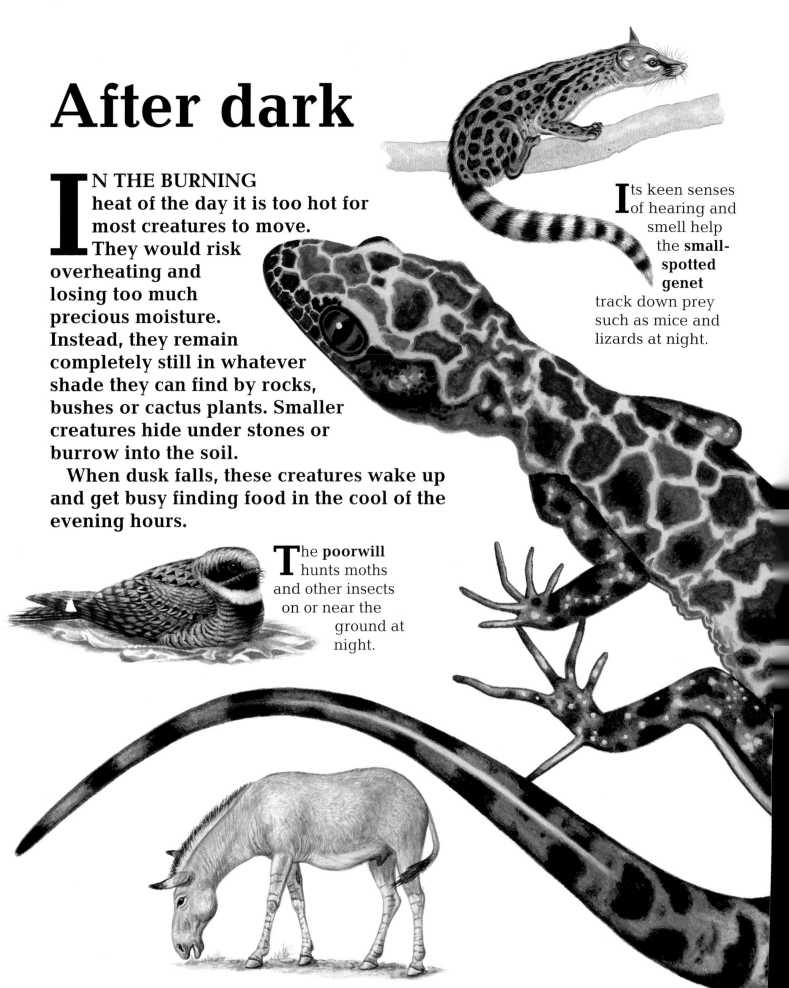

IN THE BURNING heat of the day it is too hot for most creatures to move. They would risk overheating and losing too much precious moisture. Instead, they remain completely still in whatever shade they can find by rocks, bushes or cactus plants. Smaller creatures hide under stones or burrow into the soil.

When dusk falls, these creatures wake up and get busy finding food in the cool of the evening hours.

Its keen senses of hearing and smell help the **small-spotted genet** track down prey such as mice and lizards at night.

The **poorwill** hunts moths and other insects on or near the ground at night.

In the heat of the day the **African ass** rests in the shade—if it can find any. At dusk it wanders around searching for grass and other plants in the semi-desert where it lives.

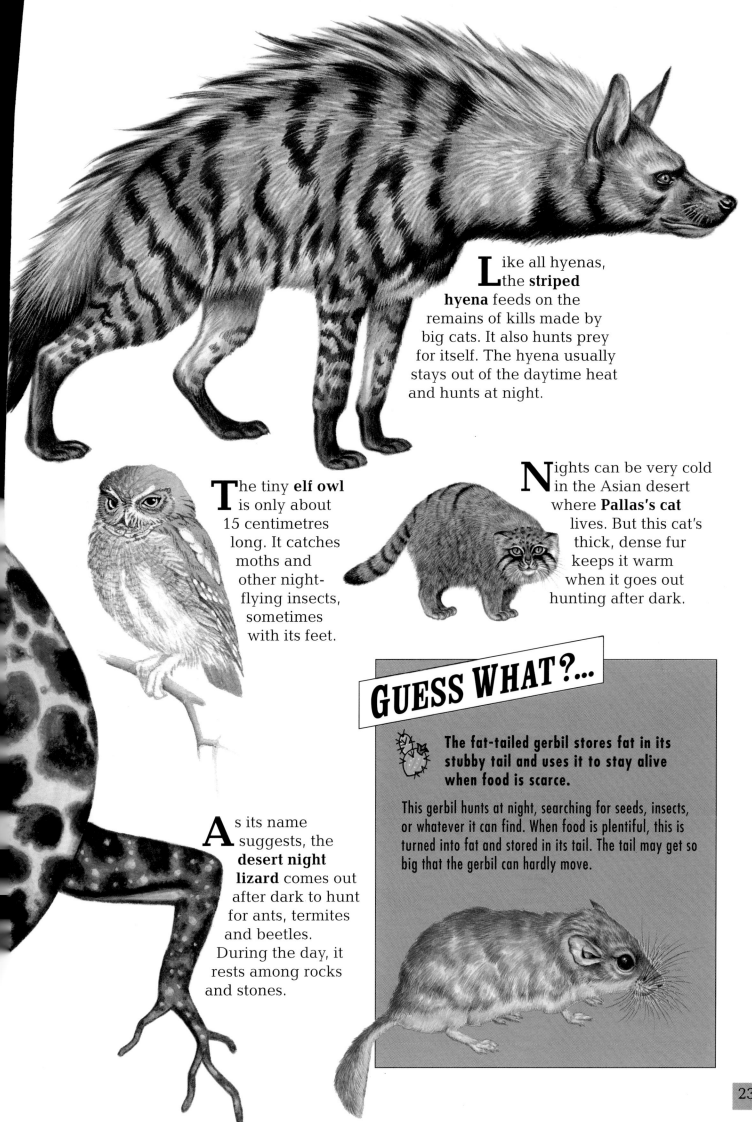

Like all hyenas, the **striped hyena** feeds on the remains of kills made by big cats. It also hunts prey for itself. The hyena usually stays out of the daytime heat and hunts at night.

The tiny **elf owl** is only about 15 centimetres long. It catches moths and other night-flying insects, sometimes with its feet.

Nights can be very cold in the Asian desert where **Pallas's cat** lives. But this cat's thick, dense fur keeps it warm when it goes out hunting after dark.

As its name suggests, the **desert night lizard** comes out after dark to hunt for ants, termites and beetles. During the day, it rests among rocks and stones.

GUESS WHAT?...

The fat-tailed gerbil stores fat in its stubby tail and uses it to stay alive when food is scarce.

This gerbil hunts at night, searching for seeds, insects, or whatever it can find. When food is plentiful, this is turned into fat and stored in its tail. The tail may get so big that the gerbil can hardly move.

Index